Dot & Jabber

and the Big Bug Mystery

Ellen Stoll Walsh

Green Light Readers

Houghton Mifflin Harcourt

Boston   New York

The illustrations in this book are cut-paper collage.
The display type was set in Berkeley Old Style.
The text type was set in Berkeley Old Style.

The Library of Congress has cataloged the hardcover edition as follows:
Walsh, Ellen Stoll
Dot & Jabber and the big bug mystery/written and illustrated by
Ellen Stoll Walsh.
p. cm.
"Companion book to Dot & Jabber and the great acorn mystery." Summary: Dot and Jabber, mouse detectives, try to solve the mystery of disappearing insects.
[1. Mice—Fiction. 2. Insects—Fiction. 3. Mystery and detective stories.] I. Title: Dot and Jabber and the big bug mystery. II. Title.
PZ7.W1675D1 2003
[E]—dc21 2002011386

ISBN: 978-0-15-216518-5 hardcover
ISBN: 978-0-544-92548-9 paper over board
ISBN: 978-0-544-92549-6 paperback

Manufactured in China
SCP 10 9 8 7 6 5 4 3 2 1

4500635246

For Ben and Katya
Для Кати и Бена

Dot and Jabber, the mouse detectives, were looking for a mystery to solve. They walked through the meadow and stopped to watch some bugs.

The mice thought they heard something. They turned to see, and when they turned back, the bugs had disappeared.

"Wow," said Jabber. "The bugs vanished. Poof!"

"They must be around here someplace," said Dot. "They couldn't have gone away so fast."

"Then they're invisible," said
Jabber. "I can't see them at all, and
I'm looking."

"Come on, Jabber," said Dot.
"This is the mystery we've been
looking for. Let's find those bugs!
We need to look for clues."

"Dot, listen," Jabber whispered.
"I think I hear one."

"One what?" said Dot.

"One clue. *Shhh*. Let's go check."
The mice crept over the hill.

"It's a sparrow," Jabber said.
"No wonder the bugs disappeared.
Sparrows eat bugs."

"Not me," the sparrow said. "I'm
going to find some berries. They
don't vanish when you want one."
And he hopped off.

"Now that the sparrow is gone," said Dot, "why don't the bugs come back?"

"They're hiding from the toad,"
said a rabbit. "Toads eat bugs too."

"Where is the toad?" said Dot.

"Hiding from things that eat toads," said the rabbit.

"I don't get it," said Jabber. "Everybody is hiding, but I don't see anyplace to hide."

"Maybe we don't know how to look," said Dot. "Let's keep searching. The bugs can't be that far away."

"They're watching us," said Jabber. "I can feel it."

"I can too," said Dot.

"This gives me goose bumps," said Jabber. "They can see us, but we can't see them. I wonder what else is out there watching us . . ."

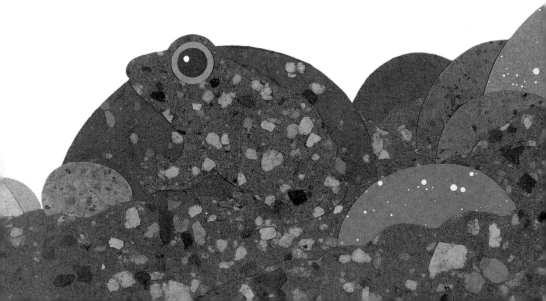

Dot caught her breath. "Jabber, quick. Something moved."

"I don't see it," said Jabber.

"Look," said Dot. "It's moving again."

Some butterflies rose from the meadow and flew away.

"Wow—butterflies!" said Jabber. "I think the butterflies are a clue. They were hiding in plain sight, and we didn't even see them. Maybe the other bugs are hiding in plain sight too."

"Oh!" said Dot. "Do you mean they're pretending to look like something else? Let's see if you're right."

"Dot," said Jabber. "Do rocks breathe?"

"Of course not," said Dot.

"Then I've found the toad," said Jabber.

"Jabber," said Dot. "I found the bugs!"

"*Shhh*," said a grasshopper.

"You're right, Dot. There are lots of bugs here!" said Jabber. "We just have to know how to look."

The grasshopper sighed. "Go ahead. Tell the toad where we are. Tell the whole world. What are a few bugs, more or less? I'm out of here."

"Wait for us!" said the other bugs.

"Well," said Dot, "the bugs have really disappeared now. But not before the great mouse detectives solved another mystery!" Dot looked around. "Jabber, where are you?"

"Try to find me," said Jabber.
"I'm hiding in plain sight!"

More About Insects and Camouflage

Most people call any insect a "bug." Dot and Jabber do too, because it's much more fun to use the word *bug* than *insect*.

However, only a limited number of insects actually belong to the bug family, including stinkbugs, bedbugs, and mealybugs. So all bugs are insects, but not all insects are bugs.

Many insects (including bugs) use camouflage to blend in with their surroundings. That means they have the same colors, shapes, or markings as the things around them. For example, a green grasshopper is hard to see next to green grass and leaves. Colorful butterflies can be tough to spot among flowers. Some moths blend in with tree bark.

Why would insects want to blend in? Their survival depends on it. Bigger creatures that want to gobble them up might not see them if they're well hidden. Those bigger creatures use camouflage too—to hide from the creature they want to eat and from the even bigger predators that want to eat *them!* So when a toad hops among rocks and leaves looking for insects to eat, its lumpy, mottled body is nearly invisible to other searching eyes. There's even a creature—the chameleon—that can change its color to blend in with its natural surroundings.

The next time you go to a meadow or park—or even your own backyard—look carefully and stay very still. The bugs will be very still, too. If you wait long enough, the bugs will move first. And like Dot and Jabber, you'll find them hiding in plain sight.